THE
GIANT

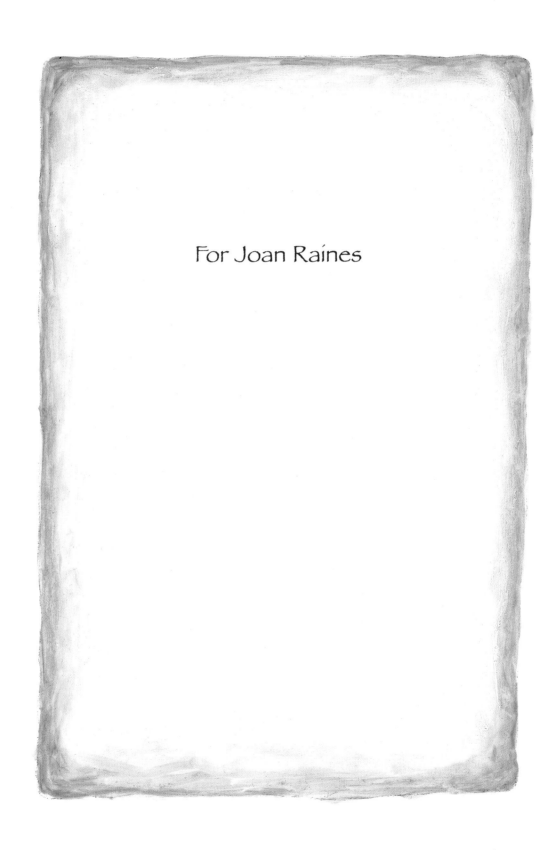

For Joan Raines

THE
GIANT

MORDICAI GERSTEIN

HYPERION BOOKS FOR CHILDREN
NEW YORK

F rom the time they were very small the three girls
had been warned to never ever go near the giant. So of
course whenever they did go, they did it secretly.

Just before dawn, whispering and giggling, they met
at the town crossroads and hurried north toward the
hills. As the sun rose they passed the last farm and went
up off the road into a field of young corn. Barefoot now,
laughing and singing, they skipped up the dew-drenched
rows toward the woods. Amelia, Reina, and Clara.

Amelia led the way, as always. Her hair fluttered behind her, black as a moonless night. You could almost see stars in it. Her violet eyes were quick and fearless. Leaping as she went, she seemed to fly.

"Oh, to leap as she does!" thought Reina, close behind. "I'm too cautious!" She leapt also, but not as high. Her yellow hair flickered like silky fire; her eyes, blueberry blue, showed flecks of gold.

"How beautiful!" thought Clara at the sight of her two leaping friends. "Like two deer! Like gazelles!" Her finespun coppery hair caught the sun's dazzle. Her ocean-green eyes shone with love.

Each girl thought the other two were the smartest, quickest, and most beautiful people in the world, and when they were together, each felt smart and quick and beautiful. Amelia, Reina, and Clara.

They danced through the dim, cool woods and out onto the bright, green meadow, shouting hellos to astonished cows. They raced up the steep hillside and zigzagged through the abandoned orchard, its trees gone wild.

"Look!" shouted Amelia. Ahead of the others, she stood on a boulder and pointed back down the hill.

Clara and Reina turned. Shielding their eyes from the level sun, they looked down into the shadowy valley. Far below they saw streets and shops and houses. Tiny automobiles and tiny people crawled along, stopping and going, and not a sound came up but the faint chug-chug-chug of the train as it made its way toward the little red station.

"It's so pretty!" said Clara. "All fresh and shiny like a doll's town."

". . . or a toy train set!" said Reina.

"Full of trained fleas!" said Amelia, and they all laughed.

"Hop, fleas!" Amelia called down to the town, waving as if conducting an orchestra.

"Hop, fleas!" they called to one another, and went hopping on up the hill, past the tumbled stones of an ancient tower, to a forgotten garden, overgrown but still blooming. They hopscotched through irises and lilies of every kind and color, up to a huge twisted apple tree growing over a broad stone wall. They climbed the rough slanted trunk and swung onto the top of the wall and stood suddenly still and breathless. At the base of the wall the hill dropped away into a ravine where, far below, hidden by brambles and mist, a rushing river could be heard. This was where their world ended and the giant's world began.

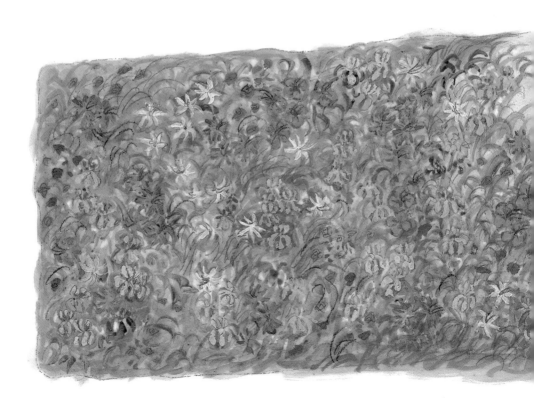

Across the ravine, on a hill called the Hump, stood the giant.

"Oh, Henry!" called Amelia. "We're here! We've come to cheer you up!"

"Dear Howard!" sang Clara. "Gentle Hector! It's us! Your special friends!"

In spite of all the times they'd come, Reina was always awed at first by the giant's immense size and stillness. He stood on the humpy brown hill like a colossus in the form of a scarecrow. A swarm of screeching starlings perched on his ears and shoulders. His expression was blank as the sky.

Swaying slightly, he stared blankly down at his sprouting garden. The girls heard the breeze flutter and flap through his shirt, a patchwork of hundreds of burlap gunnysacks, old awnings, paint-spattered tarps, faded flags, old convertible car tops, and what looked like the sails of a Spanish galleon. His vast, baggy trousers were made mostly from pieces of circus tents with pictures of elephants, fat ladies, and two-headed calves, now all but washed away. His clothes and his patchy, thatchy, yellow-brown hair, so like the grass of the hill, all fluttered in the playful breeze.

The giant stared at his garden as if he'd forgotten what it was.

"Hello again, Harry!" Reina called. "Aren't you delighted to see us?"

"We'll sing you a song, Herman," shouted Clara, "to make you smile!"

"We've come, Horatio," yelled Amelia, "to make you HAPPY!"

Trying to guess the giant's name had been Clara's idea. "If we call him by name we'll get his attention," she reasoned. So they were going through the alphabet, calling out all the names they could think of for each letter. But so far he hadn't responded. In fact, for him, the girls seemed not to exist at all. Even last fall when Amelia had thrown apples that bounced off his head and face he'd taken no notice.

"Maybe he hasn't got a name," suggested Reina.

"Or maybe," said Clara, "he's deaf, poor thing."

"Or maybe," said Reina, "we're just too small for him to see or hear. Like teeny microscopic bugs."

"We are not bugs!" said Amelia fiercely. "We are a perfect size and we are delightful! He will see us and hear us. We will brighten his life!"

"Dearest Isaac," called Clara, "won't you please give me a tiny smile or hello?"

"Please, precious Icarus," mimicked Reina, "can't you see how Clara feels about you? Even a sneeze would bring her bliss."

The girls jumped when an explosion shook dust and starlings from the giant's hair. The girls burst into laughter. The giant had sneezed.

"He sneezed for YOU!" teased Amelia, drilling a finger between Reina's ribs. "It's you he has his eye on!"

"Of course," Reina giggled, squirming away. "I'm the pretty one, but it's YOU he dreams of at night!"

"Now don't fight over him, you two," laughed Clara. "It's only fair to let HIM decide which of you he wants to marry."

"It's you! It's you!" screamed Amelia and Reina, grabbing Clara and pushing her toward the edge of the wall. "Here she is, Ira! She adores you, Isadore! She can't go on without you!"

Wrestling and tickling one another, they spun round and round, screaming and laughing.

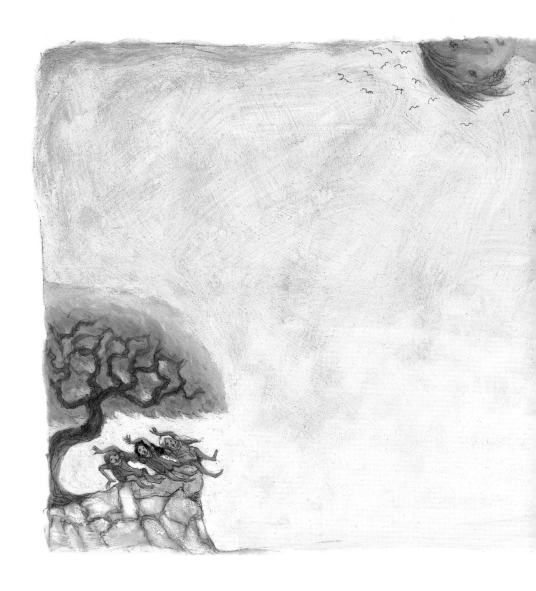

"Oh, look!" said Clara. "He's going to weed his
garden!"

The girls quickly sat in a row on the wall to watch.

After a moment they heard creaks, cracks, and explo-
sive pops: the sounds a tall tree makes when it begins to
fall. Slowly, the giant's body began to lean forward. As it
leaned, his right arm swung out and his hand—with

fingers like the roots of an uprooted oak — was lowered
toward the garden.

Cracking, creaking, and popping, the giant slanted
forward, and the girls shrank back — sure he was going
to topple over — until, with a thud that bounced them on
the wall, one of his knees hit the ground. Then, with his
great, blunt thumb and forefinger, the giant began his
weeding.

He grew large things: watermelons like green blimps, pumpkins like carriages, Hubbard squash like warty blue meteorites, rutabagas like boulders, vast cabbages, carrots full and tall as the girls themselves, and sunflowers that bloomed and blotted out the sun. But when the plants were tiny sprouts, as they were that breezy spring morning, weeding was difficult for the giant.

With enormous care he plucked a sprout, and, like a towering construction crane, raised it slowly up against his eye, pale blue like a small sky. After peering, blinking, and squinting at it, unsure if it was vegetable or weed, he swung the plant down under a bristling nostril and sniffed noisily at it, inhaling flies, bees, and sometimes a small bird. Still baffled, he swung the sprout round to his convoluted, cavelike ear and listened to it, as if it were a microscopic radio playing incredibly faint music. If he decided, finally, the plant was a weed, he parted his thumb and forefinger and watched it float to the ground. If it was a vegetable, mistakenly plucked, he sighed like a whale, dropped it into his mouth, and swallowed it with a sound like a bathtub draining.

All this made the girls laugh so hard, they had to close their eyes from time to time just to catch their breath. The laughter echoed back and forth from one to the other, till they were limp and helpless, weeping happily. There was nothing they loved better than laughing.

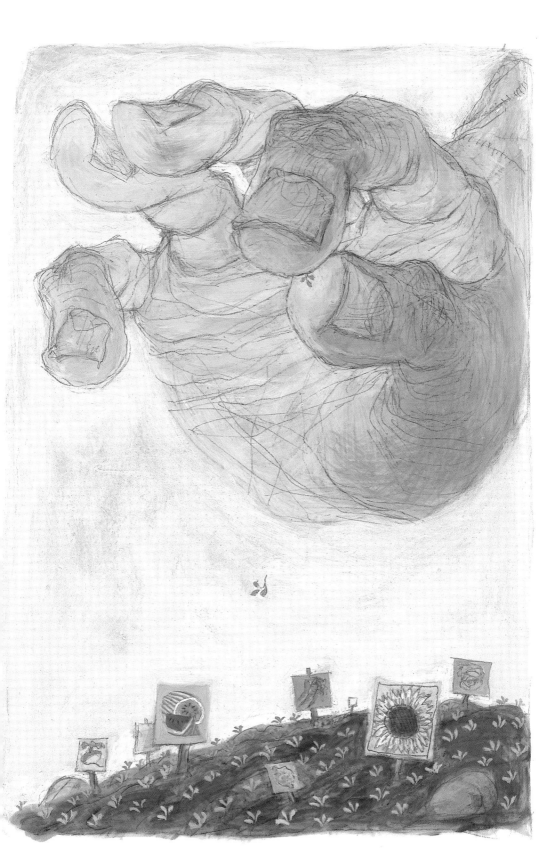

When they recovered enough to sit up and wipe their eyes, the giant was again perfectly still but in a new pose. One arm stuck out and up as if he were about to scratch his back but then forgot to. The other arm was cocked, elbow out, hand poised near his ear, which was turned toward the ravine and the girls. His eyes rolled slowly round and round, clockwise then counterclock-wise.

"He's pretending," said Amelia, "to be an apple tree with eyeballs!" Reina began laughing again, but Clara sat forward and stared.

"NO!" she cried. "Look! He hears us! For the first time! He hears us!"

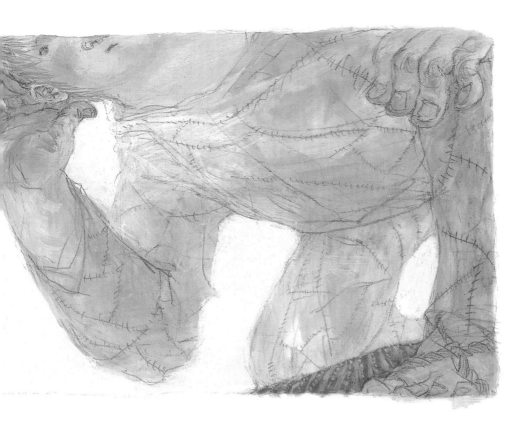

They looked and saw that it was true. The playful
breeze had blown their laughter across the ravine and
into one of the giant's enormous earth-crusted ears. He
had heard them. But he had not yet seen them.

The girls jumped up and down and waved their arms,
shouting as loudly as they could. Amelia threw handfuls
of pebbles and leaves. "Over here! Look! We're over
here! YOO-HOO!"

Creaking and popping, the giant stood to his full
height. His revolving eyes peered across the ravine. The
girls could almost see his gaze, like a searchlight, brush-
ing the branches and leaves above their heads, feeling
for them. Reina stepped back.

"Maybe . . . ," she said, ". . . maybe we shouldn't bother him. Maybe we should leave him alone now."

Amelia turned to her and laughed. "Are you afraid?" she asked.

"I know it sounds silly," said Reina, "but we don't know what he might do if he sees us. We don't really know him. Not really."

"We do," said Clara. "He's just a big, old, lonely pussycat. He'll smile and wave and know he has friends! Besides, he's way across the ravine."

The giant leaned far toward them now. He heard them and his look touched each leaf and stone around them, searching for what he heard.

"Are we really his friends?" asked Reina. "Don't we come here to laugh at him? He's a comical monster! I admit it; I've always been afraid. That's part of the fun!"

"No!" said Amelia. "I want him to know I exist! I want him to see me!"

She turned, jumped off the wall and into the old flower garden. She ran, gathering armfuls of irises, tiger lilies, daylilies, Turk's cap, and lilies of the valley, arranging them round her neck, through her button-holes and belt, and at her shoulders. She twisted honey-suckle, locust flowers, and roses into her hair, and when she jumped back onto the wall, Clara laughed and applauded.

"Wonderful!" she cried. "A walking garden!"

But Reina moved away. "Please be careful," she said. "I really think we should leave him be!"

"Oh, Arnold!" Amelia shouted to the giant, "Bill, Clyde! David! It's me, Amelia! I'm here, Edward, Frank, George! I can dance, Harry, Ishmael, Jack! I can leap! I can sing, Ken, Luke, Martin! I can do handstands and cartwheels, Norman! I can do long division in my head, and I can paint pictures, Oscar! Paul! My hair is long and black, Quincy! I can do front and back flips, Robert! I can run like the wind, Steven! And

I'm not afraid of anything, Timothy! Ulysses! Victor! Wallace! Here I am, Xavier, Yorick, Zachary! Look at me! I'm here!"

Singing and shouting, Amelia danced along the edge of the wall. On her left Reina stood pale and trembling. On her right, Clara laughed and jumped up and down clapping time. They all watched the giant.

His snuffling nostrils sniffed and flapped, and his gaze combed the air around them in ever smaller circles until, finally, it caught them.

His eyes rested on Amelia and held her, and Clara and Reina on either side were seen and held also. They all felt the weight of those boulderlike eyes, and they were unable to speak or move.

The eyes stared at them in amazement. Opening wider and wider, they began to brighten—as if lights were being turned up inside. The girls saw and felt the light increase, till—all at once—Clara realized the eyes were smiling. They were smiling at her.

The giant stepped toward them, to his edge of the ravine. His sandals, truck tires tied together with bridge cable, sent dirt and rocks tumbling into the mist below. The smile began spreading over his face, a full acre high and wide. Amelia thought it was like seeing a mountain-side smile; like watching a landscape melt like butter in a hot skillet. The girls had never been this close. They could see ripples as small animals ran through the giant's hair. They could see plants sprouting from his pores. In his ears, like terraced gardens, potato vines and small fruit trees flourished. In his mouth, crows pecked around teeth like broken gravestones in a forgotten cemetery. In the crevices around his eyes there were birds' nests, some full of new-hatched nestlings. And in his enormous eyes—eyes that held them drowning in a torrent of light—they saw themselves reflected, huddled on the wall, tiny and afraid.

The giant reached his hand out over the ravine. It came closer and closer, and the girls could see moss and ferns and dandelions growing in the cracked ridges of his hilly palm. Reina was sure she saw, behind the thumb hump, a red fox look at her with green eyes before it turned and ran up the sleeve.

When the tips of its fingernails all but touched the girls' toes, the hand stopped. Nothing moved but the breeze, and the girls heard nothing but their pounding hearts.

At that last moment, as the hand lifted to take them, Amelia plucked a purple iris from her belt and threw it into the giant's palm. Clara, as if suddenly awakened, tossed a daylily from Amelia's hair, and Reina, trembling, threw a Turk's cap. The hand paused. Gradually, the giant's gaze—like a tremendous weight—slowly slid off and away from them. He looked down into his palm. The hand began to move away. Back over the ravine, up toward his face up to nostrils like wild gloomy tunnels he slowly raised the flowers. Then he inhaled them.

The girls spun around and leapt off the wall.

They tumbled and tripped through the garden, and ran through the wild old orchard. They stumbled past the black-and-white cows and rolled down the hillside of the high meadow; dodging trees, they ran like rabbits through the woods, then burst into the cornfield— flying now, barely touching the ground—out onto the road, where they hugged one another and wept and laughed and sobbed, till there was only sobbing, and then they started to laugh again.

Holding hands, they started down the road with
Amelia in the middle, honeysuckle still tangled in her
hair, one ivory iris at her waist. Sometimes one of them
broke into tears or laughter. Sometimes one or all of
them began sobbing or giggling, as they shuffled
through the soft pale dust, reddened by the afternoon
sun. When they reached the crossroads, without a

word, they parted, and each went to her own home. Clara, Reina, and Amelia.

Each one, that evening, as she sat with her family before steaming bowls of soup, had the look of someone with a secret; but when asked, said, "Oh, nothing—it's really nothing."

And in their beds that night, each finally alone—
Reina, Clara, Amelia—each went over the events of the
day the way one examines shells and beach glass after
a visit to the sea. But these were like pieces of a shat-
tered mirror. The girls turned them carefully over and
over and wondered. And as they wondered they heard,
from far away, a sound.

It was not the train with its long, lonely whistle, nor
the call of an owl or loon, but it was like these. It was
like coyotes singing and like the ocean and the keening
wind. After a while, they realized they had heard it
every night—ever since they could remember—without
ever really hearing it. Now they knew what it was.
From way off on the humpy hill, they heard the giant
weeping.

FIRST EDITION
1   3   5   7   9   10   8   6   4   2

Library of Congress Cataloging-in-Publication Data
Gerstein, Mordicai
The giant / written and illustrated by Mordicai Gerstein — 1st ed.
p.   cm.
Summary: Three lively little girls attempt to start a friendship
with a lonely giant.
ISBN 0-7868-0131-X (trade) — ISBN 0-7868-2104-3 (lib. bdg.)
[1. Giants—Fiction.]   I. Title.
PZ7.G325Gg   1995
[Fic]—dc20   94–38650

The artwork for each picture is prepared using acrylic.

The book is set in 14-point Cochin.